Kiss Good Night, Sam

Amy Hest   illustrated by Anita Jeram

WALKER BOOKS
AND SUBSIDIARIES
LONDON · BOSTON · SYDNEY · AUCKLAND

It was a
dark and stormy night
on Plum Street.

In the little white house
Mrs Bear was putting
Sam to bed.

"Ready now, Sam?"
"Oh no," said Sam.
"I'm waiting."

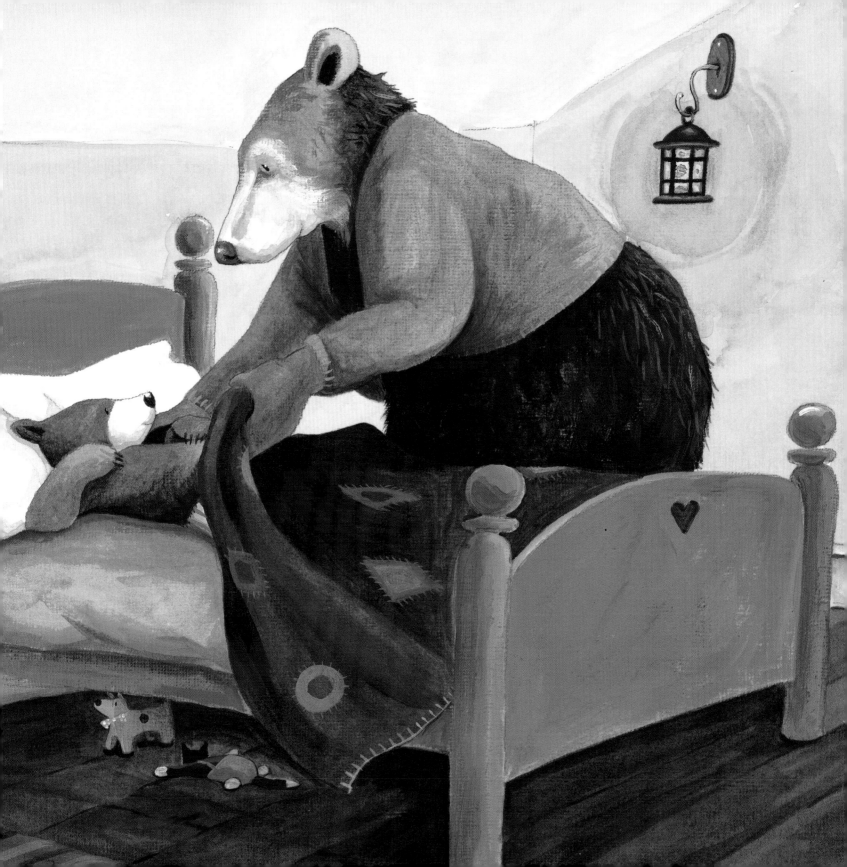

Mrs Bear sat on the bed beside Sam and they read his favourite book and they both knew all the words.

Afterwards, Mrs Bear pulled one side
of the blanket way up high under
Sam's chin, and the blanket was red.
She pulled the other side too,
tucking it under his toes like a nest.
Outside the wind blew.
Whoo, whoooo!

"Ready now, Sam?"
"Oh no," said Sam.
"I'm waiting."

Mrs Bear arranged Sam's friends in the bed and they all snuggled close in the blanket that was red. Outside the rain came down. Splat! on the roof. Splat! Splat! on the windows. The wind blew. **Whoo, whoooo!**

"Ready now, Sam?"
"Oh no," said Sam.
"I'm waiting."

Mrs Bear poured milk
in two glasses and they both
drank milk and it was warm
sliding down. Afterwards,
Mrs Bear yawned. "You must
be ready now," she said.

But Sam shook his head.
"I'm waiting," he said.

"Hmmmm," said Mrs Bear.
"Let me think. We've read
   a book and made a nest,
   arranged your friends
   and had warm milk.
   Sam," she said,
"what did I forget?"

   "You know," said Sam.

"Hmmmm," said Mrs Bear.
"Book, blanket,
friends, milk...
Book, blanket,
friends, milk..."

Sam waited.
He waited and waited.

And then at last,
Mrs Bear said,
"Oh, I know!
Kiss good night, Sam!"

And she bent way down,
kissing Sam once
and twice
and then twice more.

"Again!"
cried Sam.

And she bent way down,
kissing Sam once
and twice and
then twice more.

Outside the wind blew

and the rain came down.

In the little white house
Mrs Bear was taking out
the light, whispering,
     "Kiss good night, Sam,
        kiss good night..."

And Sam went to sleep.
On a dark and stormy night
on Plum Street.

For Sam, and you know why ~ A.H.

For Kitty ~ A.J.

First published 2001 by Walker Books Ltd
87 Vauxhall Walk, London SE11 5HJ

This edition published 2002

8 10 9

Text © 2001 Amy Hest
Illustrations © 2001 Anita Jeram

This book has been typeset in Contemporary Brush Bold

Printed in China

British Library Cataloguing in Publication Data:
a catalogue record for this book is available from the British Library

978-0-7445-8935-1

www.walker.co.uk